D0971709

TRACKS

MASON FALLS MYSTERIES

TRACKS

VANESSA ACTON

darbycreek

MINNEAPOLIS

Darby Creek
A division of Lerner Publishing Group, Inc.
241 First Avenue North
Minneapolis, MN 55401 USA

For reading levels and more information, look up this title at
www.lernerbooks.com.

Cover and interior images: AlenKadr/Shutterstock.com (texture); iStock.com/ Vectorfactory (skyline); iStock.com/bubaone (tracks); iStock.com/Fosin2 (shutter icon).

Main body text set in Janson Text LT Std 12/17.5.
Typeface provided by Adobe Systems.

Library of Congress Cataloging-in-Publication Data

Names: Acton, Vanessa, author.
Title: Tracks / by Vanessa Acton.
Description: Minneapolis : Darby Creek, [2018] | Series: Mason Falls mysteries |
Summary: When "The Kid" that high schooler Nick sees from the bus every day disappears, Nick and former friend Ava investigate to learn if something is wrong.
Identifiers: LCCN 2017029927 | ISBN 9781541501126 (lb) | ISBN 9781541501218 (pb) | ISBN 9781541501225 (eb pdf)
Subjects: | CYAC: Mystery and detective stories. | Friendship—Fiction. | Missing children—Fiction.
Classification: LCC PZ7.1.A228 Tr 2018 | DDC [Fic]—dc23

LC record available at https://lccn.loc.gov/2017029927

Manufactured in the United States of America
1-43784-33636-9/21/2017

CHAPTER 1

The Kid looked unhappy this morning. Nick watched him from the window of the school bus as it rumbled along the road that ran parallel to the train tracks. There was something about the hunch in the Kid's shoulders, the way his head ducked so low that his chin almost disappeared into his neck. "Looks like the Kid is already having a bad day," Nick remarked to Ava, who sat next to him.

Ava looked up from scrolling through the playlists on her phone. Glanced past Nick, out the window, toward the scrawny boy walking along the train tracks. Then she looked back down at her phone. "Don't be so creepy."

"I'm not being creepy. We see him every day, twice a day. Sometimes I get curious."

Ava just grunted. Nick had known her most of his life, but he still couldn't always tell what her grunts meant. To be fair, they hadn't spent much time together during the years between first and tenth grade. It was only this past year that they'd started sitting together on the bus again, now that all their real friends had cars or got rides to school. And they still didn't talk that much. Usually they just listened to music or texted their actual friends. Still, Nick sometimes wished he had a clearer idea of what she was thinking. Like now, for instance: had her grunt meant "Fair enough, curiosity's natural" or "I still think you're creepy"?

By the time Nick looked out the window again, the bus had left the Kid in its dust. Nick had to crane his neck around to see the Kid's shrinking form. There wasn't anything very distinctive about the Kid. He was skinny and small, maybe in seventh or eighth grade. He had glasses, wore a lot of gray and brown and camo-green, and carried a navy blue backpack

that usually looked painfully heavy. Nick
had seen him walking along those tracks, to
and from school, every school day since last
September. Always alone.

There had always been something vaguely
sad about it, Nick thought. But the Kid had
never looked downright *miserable* until this
morning.

I don't even know his name, Nick thought.
Ava's right. I'd better dial back the stalker thoughts.

He slipped his headphones on and listened
to music for the rest of the ride to school.

/////

That afternoon when classes were over, Nick
headed across the school parking lot to the
spot where the bus waited. When he climbed
aboard, he saw that Ava was already sitting in
their usual spot, behind Jacob and Hannah.
The four of them were the only high school
students who still regularly rode the bus. The
rest of the seats were taken up by students
from the middle school attached to Mason
Falls High School. Ava always got the window

seat on the way home, and he had it on the way to school. He made his way to the back of the vehicle—prime real estate for two of the oldest students on the bus. As little kids, he and Ava had sat together at the front of the bus that took them to and from their elementary school. At least until Jeff Groves started teasing them about being boyfriend and girlfriend.

Nick strolled down the aisle, past the rowdy middle schoolers. He didn't really know any of them. In fact, he probably knew more about the Kid than he did about any of his younger fellow passengers. He didn't even really know Jacob and Hannah, though he was pretty sure they were dating.

He slid in next to Ava and tucked his backpack under the seat as they both mumbled "Hey." Ava was buried in her phone, texting someone.

"Morino," she said, addressing him by his last name like she usually did, "you're a human male."

"Um . . . yes?" he confirmed, not sure where she was going with this.

"Explain to me why a guy would find it offensive if a girl asked him to a dance instead of the other way around."

"I assume you're asking for a friend?" Nick said. Ava had been dating Dan Ortega since freshman year.

The bus pulled out of the parking lot as Ava responded. "Yeah, Jordyn is texting me about her latest awkward conversation with Jeff Groves. He hasn't asked her to the dance yet, and she won't just ask *him* because apparently nobody's tipped her off that it's the twenty-first century."

Nick took his phone and earbuds out of his jeans pocket. "I mean, you can inform her that Kammy asked *me* to be her boyfriend, and I was more than fine with that."

"Excellent." Ava's thumbs fluttered across her screen. "That'll sway her. Jordyn thinks Kammy is *extremely cool*. Her words, not mine. Though I also like Kammy, from what I know of her."

"Uh, thanks," said Nick, untangling his earbuds. Now that he thought of it, Ava and

Kammy would probably get along really well if they hung out. But their friend groups didn't overlap, except through Nick.

The bus hit a pothole and jolted sharply. Nick braced himself against the back of the seat in front of him. They'd reached Old Creek Road, parallel to the train tracks. Nick was pretty sure it hadn't been repaved since before he was born. "Good old Jeff Groves," he said. "Remember how terrible he was in elementary school?"

"He's still terrible," said Ava mildly, looking up from her phone and glancing out the window. "He's just more ripped now. Jordyn doesn't have the best taste . . ."

Her words trailed off and she sat up straight. "Whoa. What's up with the Kid?"

Nick peered past her out the window. There were the train tracks, and there, just up ahead of the bus, was the Kid. Running full tilt.

"I don't think I've ever seen him run before," said Ava.

It was true. They'd seen the Kid walking to and from school during downpours and in sub-zero weather. He'd always been trudging along at a steady walk.

The bus rolled on down the road, catching up to the Kid and then passing him. Nick and Ava watched him until he was out of sight. And even then, Nick couldn't stop thinking about the expression in the Kid's eyes.

This time he hadn't just looked miserable. He looked terrified.

CHAPTER 2

Nick and Ava's neighborhood was on the outskirts of Mason Falls, over the train tracks and near the forest preserve. Nick got dropped off first. "See you tomorrow," he said to Ava, as usual, and she responded with "Yup," as usual. Neither of them had said anything else about the Kid. Nick couldn't tell if Ava was still thinking about him or if she was just distracted by her friend Jordyn's texts.

Nick was definitely still thinking about him, though. The look on the Kid's face had been so frantic, so haunted. Something awful must have happened to him today.

As he headed inside, Nick noticed the FOR SALE sign in front of the house next door. Josh's old house. Josh's family had been gone for three years, but that house just kept changing hands. Who were the people who'd moved in last summer? The Wilkersons, the Wilkinsons, something like that? *Oh well—they were never friendly, and if they're not sticking around I guess I don't need to remember their names.*

In the kitchen, he opened the fridge and grabbed one of the yogurt containers his dad always stocked. He wondered how Josh was doing. Nick, Ava, and Josh had shared a lot of playdates as little kids. Lots of bicycle races, lots of trips to the community pool, lots of squirt gun fights and snowball fights and fights over the TV remote. That had all trickled off once Josh's parents had sent him to a private school in fourth grade. The three of them had drifted apart, made their own friends. Or at least, Nick and Ava had made their own friends. But Josh had still wanted to hang out with Nick on weekends, so from time to time

Nick would play a video game with him or something. They'd lost touch after Josh moved at the end of middle school, and the last time Nick had looked for him on social media, he'd come up empty.

Why am I thinking about this now? he asked himself. *Time to focus on what's really important, like eating this yogurt.* He tried to shrug off the memories of his long-gone neighbor—along with the nagging uneasiness he felt about the Kid.

/////

The next morning, Nick was halfway through a math assignment he'd forgotten to do when Ava joined him on the bus. "Cutting it a little close there?" she asked, nodding at the open textbook and papers in his lap.

"Yeah, it totally slipped my mind last night. How are you?"

"Tired of hearing Jordyn talk about Jeff Groves. Otherwise fine. At least it's Friday."

This was about as much conversation as they usually had. Back at the beginning of the school year, Ava had walked over to his seat and said, "How's it going, Morino? Cool if I sit here?" He'd stuttered out a surprised "Uh, sure?" And that had set the tone for their interactions ever since.

For the next few minutes, Nick went back to his homework and Ava listened to her music. But when they reached Old Creek Road, Nick looked up. There were the tracks, stretching out as far as he could see in either direction. Just the tracks—nothing and no one else.

"Hey," he said to Ava. "Where's the Kid?"

Ava dutifully looked out the window. "Clearly not here."

"That seems weird, doesn't it?"

Ava shrugged, though Nick saw her dark eyebrows furrow. "He could be home sick."

Nick shook his head, a feeling of alarm building in his chest. "He's never missed a day of school. Remember last fall when he was sneezing for like a week straight?"

"I do not remember that because I haven't been tracking his every move."

"I just happened to notice it, Ava. There's nothing wrong with *noticing* things."

Ava seemed to catch the note of anger in his voice. She shot him a surprised look and took out both her earbuds, a clear sign that he had her full attention. "Okay, relax, I didn't mean to offend you. I just haven't been paying as much attention to him as you have, that's all I'm saying."

"Well, I don't think he's the type of kid who skips school even if he's sick."

"Maybe he had to get his wisdom teeth out."

"He's too young to need his wisdom teeth out."

"Well, maybe his family went on a trip. Or a relative died and he's at the funeral. There are a million valid reasons for him to miss a day of school. Or he could've gotten a ride for once! And anyhow, it's none of our business."

"But what if he's in some kind of trouble?"

"What kind of trouble? Like you think he's been kidnapped or something?"

"I don't know! It's possible, right? It happens."

"Seriously, Nick?" The use of his first name startled him. She generally called him Morino. "Come on, calm down. I'm sure the Kid is fine. You're making way too big a deal of this."

Nick sighed and shook his head, searching for a way to explain himself. "It's just—the way he was running yesterday. And the way he looked so panicked. It just—I don't know—I guess it worries me. Maybe it's dumb, but I can't help it."

Ava's expression softened. "Yeah, he did seem pretty freaked out yesterday. But it's not like we know him, Nick. It's not like we're responsible for him. We don't even know who he is. So unless we hear that some thirteen-year-old kid from Mason Falls has been reported missing or something, I don't see how there's much we can do."

Nick slumped in his seat. "Yeah, you're right."

"Anyway," added Ava, "he'll probably be back on Monday. He's probably fine." Which wasn't the same as what she'd said a moment ago—*I'm sure the Kid is fine*. Even Ava had to admit that it was impossible to be sure of that. And Monday seemed like a long ways away.

/////

Nick wasn't expecting to see Ava at lunchtime. He'd known they had the same lunch period, but she always sat with her friends way on the other side of the cafeteria. So when he saw her walking over to his table, he wasn't sure how to react.

"What are you doing here?" he blurted out. Which was definitely not the ideal response.

"Uh, hi to you too," she said dryly. "Hey, Kammy." She nodded to the others at the table. "Gentlemen."

"Ava, right?" said Kammy, smiling. "How's it going?"

"Fine, thanks. I just wanted to give Nick this." She held out a large book with a hard black cover.

Nick raised his eyebrows. "Last year's school yearbook?"

"I borrowed it from Dan's friend who's on the yearbook staff," Ava explained. "Thought maybe you could find the Kid in there, and figure out who he is, and then check that everything's okay with him."

"Oh," said Nick, still caught off guard. "That, uh—that's a great idea. Thanks." He took the book from her.

"Who's the Kid?" asked Kammy.

"It's a long story," said Nick.

Ava shot him a skeptical look. "Actually it's not. There's this middle school kid Nick and I see walking along the train tracks every day when our bus drives by. We didn't see him this morning and Nick was worried about him."

"Oh," said Kammy. "That's super sweet. Do you want to sit down and look through the yearbook with him? We have room."

Ava raised her eyebrows at Nick.

"Oh, for sure," said Nick, scooting over to make room on the bench. "I mean, if you want to."

"Thanks, Kammy," said Ava in the same dry tone, though she was still looking at Nick. She sat down on the bench between Nick and his friend Renzo, and Nick set the

15

book on the table between them. Embossed across the cover were the words MASON FALLS MIDDLE SCHOOL AND HIGH SCHOOL YEARBOOK. Nick flipped to the class pictures and started scanning faces.

No Kid, no Kid, still no Kid . . .

"Wait, there he is!" Ava's finger shot out and jabbed at a picture near the bottom of a page showing last year's seventh graders.

Nick looked down at the serious-faced boy with the messy hair and uncool glasses. "Yeah, that's definitely him." He read the name listed under the photo. "Marcus Hall."

"Who's this kid again?" asked Renzo.

Nick didn't look up. "We're not sure yet."

CHAPTER 3

Marcus Hall didn't seem to have a social media presence. Nick spent the rest of his lunch hour on his phone, looking for any trace of him. No luck. Maybe Marcus's parents were strict about enforcing the actual age restrictions for that stuff.

While Nick was absorbed in his internet search, Ava took the borrowed yearbook and went back to her own lunch table. But Kammy and the others at Nick's table had taken an interest in the situation now, so Nick turned to his girlfriend and said, "Kammy, your brother's in eighth grade, right?"

"Yeah. I don't think Kayden's friends with this Marcus kid, though. He doesn't look familiar to me, and Kayden has his friends over all the time."

"But he might know him a little," Nick murmured, more to himself than to Kammy. "Or at least know someone else who does. This school isn't that big." Lunch was ending, so he put his phone away and picked up his tray. "The middle school kids have their lunch hour right after this, right?"

"Yeah," said Kammy as they stood up and carried their trays to the trash cans. "You planning to quiz my little brother about your mystery kid?"

Nick shrugged. "Well, next period is my free study hour, so . . . maybe?"

"This Marcus guy must've looked *really* upset yesterday if you're that worried about him."

"He did," Nick insisted. *Did he, though? Or am I blowing this whole thing out of proportion?*

"Well, Ava seems cool," Kammy remarked. "I didn't realize you two hung out."

"We don't," Nick said quickly. "I mean, just on the bus."

Kammy laughed at the expression on his face. "Will you chill? What, you think I'm going to be jealous?"

"It isn't that," stammered Nick, though maybe it partly *was* that. Didn't girlfriends get nervous about that kind of thing?

"You're not jealous when I hang out with Renzo," Kammy pointed out.

"To be fair," said Renzo in the background, "I'm not into the ladies. I'm a very safe bet as a platonic friend."

Kammy rolled her eyes. "Don't be obnoxious, Renzo. It's not like *you* don't have platonic *guy* friends." She turned back to Nick. "My point is, I like Ava. Tell her she's welcome to hang out with us sometime. You should invite her to my thing tomorrow night, actually. And meanwhile don't bother Kayden too much with this little manhunt of yours."

/////

Kayden did not know Marcus Hall. But Kayden's friend Tyler did. "Yeah, he's in my English class," Tyler said as Nick sat awkwardly at a table full of eighth graders. "He wasn't there today, though."

"Yeah?" Nick thought back to his list of reasons that Marcus might have been MIA this morning and mentally crossed off *He could've gotten a ride to school.* "Does that happen a lot?"

Tyler shrugged, then frowned as he actually thought about the question. "Actually, I don't think he's *ever* missed school. That's pretty freakish, isn't it?"

It was Nick's turn to shrug. "I'm guessing you don't know him that well?"

"Nah. Sometimes I'll see him at the skateboard park on weekends, but he never skates with us. Doesn't even have a board. Just takes pictures of the equipment with his fancy camera."

"Do you know who his friends are?"

"Uh—I don't know if he has any friends. He usually sits over there." Tyler dismissively waved a hand toward a corner table. About a dozen kids, mostly boys, sat at it. They were spread out, not talking, heads bowed over their food.

Aw, man, thought Nick, his stomach dropping a little. *A misfit table.*

He thanked Tyler and Kayden for talking to him, then headed over to the table of silent boys. "Um, hey there," he said to the group at large. "Sorry to bother you guys, but does anybody here know Marcus Hall?"

A handful of heads rose. A few eighth graders eyed him suspiciously. "Who are you?" demanded one of them.

"I'm Nick. I'm a—neighbor of Marcus's. I heard he wasn't at school today and I wanted to check to see if he's doing okay."

Silence. Nick tried again. "Do any of you have his number?"

Several boys answered by shaking their heads. Some just gave Nick *Are you serious?* looks.

"So—none of you are close friends with him?" Nick asked, though he'd already guessed the answer.

Most of the boys who were still even paying attention to him shook their heads.

Nick was about to give up and go to study hall when one boy spoke up. "If you find him, tell him Wyatt Rosen says thanks for throwing me under the bus today."

"Uh . . . will he know what you mean by that?"

The boy sat up straight, full of dignified outrage. "We were paired up to work on a project for history class. I had to do my half of the presentation all by myself. It was *agony*. Coward probably skipped just because he didn't have his half ready."

Nick was pretty sure Wyatt Rosen had never scrambled to do last night's homework on the way to school. He'd probably be working for Wyatt Rosen someday. But right now he had more questions for this kid. "Is that the kind of thing he normally does?"

"Well—no. I don't think I remember him ever missing school. Even when he *wasn't* prepared for a class."

"And it wasn't an excused absence? Like, the teacher didn't already know he'd be out? His parents didn't call him in sick or pull him out for a family emergency or anything like that?"

"Not that I know of. The teacher called his name during attendance and then was like, 'Whoa, that's a first.' And then"—he returned to his main point—"I had to do our presentation *by myself.*"

Another boy chimed in. "I don't think Marcus's parents are the kind of parents who'd even remember to call the school if he stayed home. They're always working."

"Yeah, that's true," said another kid. "We went to the same elementary school. I remember that his parents never came to our stupid sing-along assemblies or whatever. And in sixth grade there was this big art show and Marcus had a whole poster board display with photos he'd taken, and you could tell he'd put a lot of work into it. It even won a prize. But then the teacher was like, 'Do you want to take this home so your family can see it?' and he was like, 'Nah, they're never home anyway.' I mostly remember because a couple of idiots teased him about the title of his project, and he didn't even seem to notice because he was obviously thinking about his parents not being there."

"Oh yeah, I remember that," said yet another guy. "Didn't he call it *Making My Mark on the World*? Something dumb like that? And then Garrett and Joel kept calling him Making My Marcus for like a month afterward, until they figured out he kind of liked it . . ."

At that point the conversation took a sharp turn toward what jerks Garrett and Joel were. Nick thanked them and excused himself, figuring he'd gotten all the useful information he would get.

This is bleak, Nick thought as he walked away from the table. *A kid with no friends, busy parents, and an obnoxious history project partner. I would've skipped school plenty of times if I were him.*

So if none of that had stopped Marcus from coming to school before, why was he absent today?

CHAPTER 4

In the margins of his math notebook, Nick wrote down his list of *Things That Could Explain The Kid's Disappearance.*

- *sick (parents would've called the school)*
- *family reasons (same)*
- *didn't feel like showing up (unlikely)*
- *avoiding history presentation (unlikely)*
- *victim of tragic accident on the way to school*
- *on the run from the law*
- *on the run from family (family could be shady)*
- *witnessed a crime (now being relocated by witness protection)*
- *abducted by aliens (grow up, Morino)*
- *abducted by people*

It wasn't the kind of list he could expect anyone else to take seriously. But at the moment, it felt more urgent than the math lesson.

/////

At the end of the day, Ava didn't look up from her phone when Nick sat down next to her on the bus. "Hey," said Nick, like he always did. She only grunted in response. Not a great start.

Nick cleared his throat and tried to keep his voice casual. "Sorry about the way I acted at lunch. It was just kind of weird, you know— seeing my worlds collide."

Ava kept her eyes on her phone but raised her eyebrows. "You mean the bus counts as a separate world?"

"I mean—kind of. It's normally the only place we, uh, hang out." To use Kammy's words. "So it threw me off to see you around the people I *actually* hang out with."

She sighed and finally looked up at him. "You know, sometimes I think you never got over Jeff Groves teasing you about being my boyfriend in, like, fifth grade. *That's* when we stopped hanging out. When you got embarrassed to be seen with me."

"I was never embarrassed—"

"You were. It's normal, I guess." She shrugged, but not convincingly. "But it was a long time ago and I kind of thought you'd matured enough that you wouldn't mind talking to me in public."

"I—I *don't* mind talking to you in public! I told you, I was just surprised."

"Whatever. Did you find out anything about Marcus Hall?"

"Uh, a little . . ." He recapped his conversations with the eighth graders.

Ava listened with a thoughtful expression. "So it does officially seem strange that Marcus suddenly missed school out of nowhere, for the first time ever. But the school would've called his parents about an unreported absence. And if his parents don't know where he is, they could always call the police."

"Don't you have to wait twenty-four hours before you can officially report someone missing?" Nick said.

"I don't think that's actually true. Anyway, there are still plenty of logical, non-disastrous reasons for him to not be at school. Reasons that don't involve him being kidnapped and needing you to rescue him."

"I'm not out to *rescue* him," said Nick, suddenly feeling defensive again.

"So what are you doing? Just prying into a random kid's life for fun?"

"No! I just—" He cut himself off, not wanting to make Ava think he was being ridiculous. Well, even *more* ridiculous.

"What were you about to say?" She made a "go ahead" gesture with her hand.

"Nothing, just . . . Marcus kind of reminds me of Josh, that's all."

Ava's eyes widened. She clearly hadn't been expecting Nick to bring up their old friend. "This is about Josh Adler?"

Nick shifted his weight uncomfortably. "I mean, it's not *about* him. But I did kind of always wonder—if things would've been different for him if I'd been a better friend. If I'd paid attention, noticed that he was lonely . . . maybe the Adlers wouldn't have even moved."

Ava gaped at him. "Hold on. The way I remember it, the Adlers moved because Mrs. Adler got a better job. It had nothing to do with you."

"That was one reason. But I remember hearing Josh's parents tell my dad that they also thought Josh needed a change of scene. And even if they would've moved anyway, I still wish that I hadn't ignored him, that I'd been there for him. At least maybe he wouldn't have been so unhappy while he was here. So yeah, I guess I do feel guilty about it."

Ava sighed. "We were kids, Nick. We were friends when we were little because we were the same age, our houses were close, and it was convenient for our parents. It's not your fault that Josh had trouble making other friends. It's not your fault he was unhappy."

"I know, but I still wish I'd made more of an effort. And maybe that's part of why I'm so worried about Marcus. I'd hate to think that nobody was looking out for him when he needed it."

Ava was silent for a long time as the bus rattled down Old Creek Road. Finally she said, "Okay. So how are we going to track down Marcus Hall?"

CHAPTER 5

"I wish he had some kind of online presence," Nick told Ava. "Then we could at least see if he'd posted something in the last day or so."

"That would be helpful," Ava agreed. "If he'd been sharing animal videos we could be fairly sure he hadn't been kidnapped."

"Wait a minute." Nick pulled out his phone. "Everybody said Marcus takes a lot of photos. And he's proud of them. So he probably uploads them somewhere . . ." He pulled up a popular photo-sharing app.

Ava looked over his shoulder at his phone screen. "You didn't look for him here earlier?"

"I did, but just under his real name. I'm going to try something else." Nick typed *Making My Marcus* into the search bar. A profile instantly popped up. "And there he is."

"Nice!" Ava pulled the phone toward her so that they could both comfortably see it. Nick clicked on the most recent photo Marcus had posted.

"Well, he probably wasn't kidnapped as of 10:48 this morning," Ava said, noting the time stamp on the post.

"Yeah, but where did he take this?"

The photo showed a splash of purple and blue spray-painted graffiti on a concrete surface. The shape of a bird, trailed by curving, curling lines that might represent wind.

"No idea," said Ava. "That's some pretty cool graffiti, though. What else has he photographed recently?"

Nick went back to the account's home page and scrolled through the other pictures. Over the past few months, Marcus had posted photos of the train tracks at various angles, with different filters. There were more bits of graffiti

and some black-and-white images that were
so shadowy and zoomed in that Nick couldn't
really tell what they were showing. He did spot
a couple photos of the old house on Cherry
Road and different spots on the school grounds
like the track field and the baseball diamond.
Marcus had also taken a lot of nature pictures:
close-ups of plants, views of the sky through a
canopy of tree branches, that kind of stuff.

"Looks like he spends a lot of time in the
forest preserve," said Ava. "See, there's the
Mason Creek bridge—and the falls."

The town of Mason Falls was named after
a picturesque little waterfall along Mason
Creek. Nick had taken countless school field
trips there over the years. But Ava was right—
Marcus seemed to spend a lot of his free time
in that area. Judging by the time stamps on
the photos, he'd been in the forest preserve last
Saturday, and the weekend before that, and
several weekday afternoons within the past
few months.

"How would you feel about taking a walk
to Mason Creek?" Nick asked Ava.

Ava stared silently at the photo, lost in thought. For a second Nick expected her to tell him once again that he was getting carried away. But finally she nodded. "Let's do it."

CHAPTER 6

They both got off the bus at Nick's house. Nick's dad, who got home early on Fridays, was outside mowing the lawn with his dinky manual push mower. "Hey, Dad," Nick said. "We're going to the forest preserve. I'll be back by dinnertime."

Mr. Morino let the little manual mower slide to a stop. "Is that our Ava? Long time no see!"

"Hi, Mr. Morino," said Ava brightly. "Nick and I are just heading over to the falls for a little bit."

Nick added, "I guess it's pointless to ask if I can take the car?"

Mr. Morino gave a dramatic sigh. He said to Ava, "Ever since he got his license I hear this from him fifteen times a day. Can I take the car for this, can I take the car for that. Nothing wrong with a good stretch of the legs, right?"

Typical Dad, thought Nick with an inward sigh. Mr. Morino was always trying to reduce his carbon footprint. That meant having an energy-efficient car that he never let Nick drive. And stashing all their old computers, phones, and TVs in the basement to "keep them out of a landfill." And, as of right now, using a manual lawn mower instead of an electric one.

"Sure," said Ava, smiling in agreement with Mr. Morino. "It's a short walk to the forest preserve anyway."

Nick's dad beamed at her. "That's the spirit! Feel free to leave your backpacks inside before you go. Front door's unlocked. How are your parents, Ava?"

Ava chatted with Mr. Morino while Nick dumped their backpacks in the front hall. As he came back outside and shut the door behind him, he heard his dad say, "And you know, you're welcome to join us for dinner . . ."

Ava smiled back at him. "I'd love to. Thanks, Mr. Morino. See you in a couple hours."

As they set off toward the forest preserve, Ava glanced sideways at Nick. "You don't mind if I stay for dinner, do you? I remember your dad being a really good cook."

"Of course I don't mind," said Nick quickly.

"You look like you mind."

"Well, I *don't*," he snapped, which probably wasn't very convincing. "It just kind of came out of nowhere."

Ava pursed her lips and quickened her pace. "Here's what I don't get," she said. "If you still feel guilty about not being a better friend to Josh, why don't you want to be friends with *me* again?"

"I do want to be friends with you again."

"You're not acting like it. You get spooked every time I happen to cross paths with somebody else in your life."

Nick didn't have a good explanation for her. "I'm sorry," was the best he could manage. "I don't mean to act that way."

"I won't have dinner at your house if it makes you uncomfortable," she said flatly. "And if you'd rather investigate Marcus Hall's disappearance—*theoretical* disappearance—by yourself, I can just go home right now."

"I would really like your help," Nick said quietly. "And you should totally stay for dinner too, if you want."

Ava sighed impatiently and didn't respond.

/////

The forest preserve was beautiful in spring. Nick and Ava tramped silently down one of the main trails through the woods, weaving among thick-trunked trees. Nick had his phone out so he could compare what he was seeing to the images captured in Marcus's photo stream.

Most of those photos showed flowering plants or tree bark or animals. Not super location-specific. The only real landmark they had to work with was the creek. So they took the trail that led in that direction.

"Should we call out his name or something?" Nick wondered out loud.

Ava scrunched up her face. "Ehhh. Seems a little melodramatic. Especially considering how big this park is. And the fact that we're not even sure he's been here today. Let's just look around and see if we find anything, for a start."

They reached the stone bridge that arched over the creek. Nick followed Ava about halfway across the bridge. Then she paused and looked down at the rushing water. "Still running high from the rain earlier this week," she noted.

More possibilities flitted into Nick's mind. Marcus losing his footing somewhere along the creek, falling in, getting swept along . . . *Don't be so morbid*, he told himself sternly. But the fact that Ava had mentioned the water level made him suspect she was having the same grim thoughts.

They left the bridge, and Ava hopped over the low iron fence that was supposed to keep people away from the creek's edge. "Whoa! What are you doing?" said Nick.

"You were looking at the same photos I was," she said over her shoulder. "That graffiti could be on the underside of the bridge. I want to check."

Nick hesitated a moment, then hoisted himself over the fence and followed her.

They edged their way along the underbrush that bordered the creek. Being this close to the fast-flowing water made Nick slightly sick to his stomach. But he reminded himself that Mason Creek wasn't *that* deep, and he wasn't alone. Worst-case scenario, if he somehow ended up in the water, Ava could pull him out.

They ducked under the low arch of the bridge and examined the stone. There was plenty of graffiti on it, but mostly of the *X hearts Y* type. "Hey," said Nick, "was this you and Dan?" He pointed to a lower section, where someone had carved:

$$DO + AF = \infty$$

"Oh yeah," said Ava with a laugh. "Dan

was really into the infinity symbol freshman year. And really into dumb stunts like tagging bridges in public parks. He's over it now. But yeah, he brought me here once. That's how I knew about the graffiti under here."

"Dan's always seemed like a cool guy," said Nick, feeling as if he should say something.

"Yeah, he's great. I bet you two would get along well."

Nick suddenly remembered Kammy's instructions to invite Ava to her place this weekend. But now didn't really seem like the time to bring that up. Instead he went back to studying the stone underside of the bridge.

No sign of the bird with its swirling trail of color. "Well, so much for that," sighed Ava. "Let's try the falls."

They climbed back over the fence and returned to the trail.

The falls themselves weren't very imposing. Pretty, but fairly low-key—not exactly in the running to be named a wonder of the world. The modest stream of water flowed off a tall rock formation and sort of gently absorbed itself into the creek. The rock formation though—*that* was imposing. A carefully maintained, zig-zagging footpath provided the safest, least steep route to the top. It also took almost half an hour to climb because it was so crooked and full of detours. The faster way to reach the top was to scale the bare rock face. The park service did not recommend this. Cautionary signs were scattered all along the official trail. Signs like:

STAY ON PATH.

DO NOT LEAVE PATH.

DO NOT DISTURB ROCK FORMATION.

He almost wondered if it would have been easier for them to just cut right to the point. Maybe with something like:

FOR REAL, IT'S DANGEROUS.

STAY ON THIS NICE PATH WE MADE FOR YOU.

P.S. DO NOT LITTER.

At least once a year, somebody dislocated an elbow or broke an ankle by ignoring the park service's signs.

This was enough to keep Nick and Ava on the official path.

Until Ava stopped in her tracks and said, "Look." Nick strained to see what she was pointing at. His eyes snagged on a small object sitting on a jutting piece of rock about thirty feet away from the footpath. Late-afternoon sun glinted off the object. When the clouds shifted, Nick was able to see it clearly.

It was a cell phone.

CHAPTER 7

Two seconds later Nick and Ava were off the path, picking their way across the slabs of rock. Ava reached the phone first. She scooped it up and squinted at the screen as she pressed the power button. "Battery's dead."

"Do you think it's Marcus's?" Nick asked.

"No way to know if we can't even turn it on."

"But if it is his," Nick said, "that would mean he's definitely been here today. And if he left his phone here and didn't come back for it, he really *could* be in trouble."

"Agreed," said Ava grimly. She tucked the phone into her pocket. "Now might be a good time to start calling his name."

"Should we go back to the path?"

Ava patted her bulging pocket. "Whoever left this phone here wasn't on the path."

They didn't go back to the path. Instead they crept along the sloping rocks, yelling above the sound of the rushing waterfall. "Marcus? Marcus! MARRRRRRRRCUSSSSSSS."

After about a minute of this, Nick happened to look down.

From a distance, the waterfall had looked peaceful, unthreatening. But up close—well, not so much. The water crashed down with a deafening rush and plunged into the creek at breakneck speed. *If you lost your footing up here,* he thought, *you'd have a long fall into some pretty fast-moving water.*

He tried not to focus on that. "Marcus? Marcus Halllllll!"

That was when Ava's foot slipped.

CHAPTER 8

Nick didn't have time to react. He just watched it happen. One second Ava was standing in front of him, and the next second her foot went out from under her, and she was pitching sideways and downward. "Whoa!" she shouted, thrusting out her arms, but it was too late for her to regain her balance. She landed hard on her side, on the rock she'd been standing on, and then she started to slide—toward the edge of the rock and the water below.

"Ava!" Nick felt as if he were watching this happen in slow motion, but *he* could only move in real time. His hand shot forward, but he wasn't remotely close enough to reach Ava.

This was the kind of thing he'd been afraid would happen to Marcus. But instead, Ava was the one in danger. Ava was the one who needed him—the one he'd let down.

Ava didn't actually slide very far, though. She caught herself on the rock ledge before she slipped completely off. For a moment her feet dangled freely over the edge, but then she tucked in her knees and managed to pull herself forward. By now Nick was scrambling toward her. He felt his shoes slide on the mud-slick ground—easy to see how Ava had lost her footing.

A moment later he was crouching next to her. He grabbed her by the arms and hauled her another few feet away from the drop.

"Are you okay?!" Nick was breathing hard, as though *he* were the one who'd almost gone over that ledge.

Ava slowly sat up, reeling in a deep breath. "I'm fine."

"We need to get back on the path," Nick said unsteadily. "It's too dangerous to stay over here. If Marcus is still around here, we'll have to try to spot him from a safer place."

Ava nodded and carefully got to her feet. Her whole left side was covered in mud, and the palms of her hands were pretty scraped up. Nick saw that her hands were shaking a little as she tried to brush off her jeans. But other than that she didn't seem any worse for wear. "Yeah. I mean, we haven't seen, like, a body or anything." Nick suppressed a shudder. So they *had* been thinking along the same lines.

"And if he's hiding somewhere close by, we're probably not the best people to search this area," Ava went on. "Let's get back to your place and see if we can power up this phone. I bet the power cord for your phone will work on it. Then we can find out if it really does belong to Marcus. And if it does, we can contact his family and let them know we've got it."

She didn't look nearly as shaken up as Nick felt. As they made their way back to the path, Nick couldn't help thinking about what might've happened. If she hadn't gotten a handhold so quickly, if she hadn't been able to stop herself from sliding all the way off the rock . . .

They ducked under the railing that ran along the protected path. Instead of continuing toward the top of the falls, they headed back down.

"Ava, I'm really sorry," Nick blurted out.

"Sorry about what? It's not your fault that I slipped."

He took a deep breath. "Remember when you asked me why I wasn't acting like I wanted to be friends?"

"You mean like forty-five minutes ago? Way back then?" Ava asked with a sarcastic tone. "Yeah, it's hazy but I think I can retrieve the memory if I concentrate."

"I'm trying to have a serious conversation with you here."

"Yeah, I got that vibe. Go ahead."

"Well, you know how your friend Jordyn doesn't want to ask Jeff Groves to the dance? Like, she wants to go to the dance with him but she doesn't know how to make it happen?"

"Not really sure where you're going with this, but sure."

"The thing is, I've never had any close friends who are girls. For a long time it didn't seem cool, and now it's just habit—it just kind of worked out that way. I've never brought a girl home for dinner except Kammy, my actual girlfriend. My lunch table is full of dudes, plus Kammy. On weekends I'm with those guys, unless I'm with Kammy."

"I'm seeing the pattern," she said dryly.

He pressed on. "I want us to be friends again, but I don't really know how to do that. I guess in theory it's not any different than being friends with Renzo or Owen or whoever, but I'm just not used to it. That's why I keep acting so weird, I guess."

For a moment the only sound was their feet crunching on the gravel of the path.

"So, what you're saying is . . . this really is all Jeff Groves's fault."

Nick laughed. "Uh—sure. Yeah, definitely blame him and not me."

She shook her head and grunted. Nick wasn't totally sure what that grunt meant, but he could tell it *didn't* mean she was still angry with him.

/////

They didn't talk the rest of the way home.
Both of them were focused on walking quickly
and figuring out what to do next. Back at
Nick's place, Ava handed Nick the mystery
phone. "Here, see if your power cord will fit
it." She ducked into the bathroom to rinse off
some of the grime from her fall. Nick said a
quick hello to his dad, who was busy in the
kitchen, and then headed to his room. After a
few minutes of scrambling around, he found
his phone cord. It didn't even come close to
fitting the dead phone.

Nick let out a frustrated groan. Now that
he looked at the phone more closely, it was
clearly an old-school model. Its whole shape was
different from the phones he and his friends
had, and . . . *Is that an actual keyboard?* As he
fiddled with the phone, it slid apart into two
separate panels—one for the screen and one for
an old-fashioned keypad with tiny buttons.

*Wait a minute—didn't Kayden's friend Tyler
say that Marcus had a fancy phone? This would
definitely not qualify.*

He frowned, trying to remember their conversation. *Maybe that wasn't what he said. Or maybe this isn't Marcus's phone at all.*

There was only one way to find out. He had to find a charger that would work on it.

CHAPTER 9

Nick usually tried to avoid his basement as much as possible. His dad just used it to store junk he wasn't willing to throw away. Stacked trunks, cardboard boxes, and rubber tubs snaked from one end of the room to the other. Nick edged his way along the narrow walkway between two uneven rows of trunks. Somewhere in here his dad had a box full of old phones and their chargers.

It took him about seven minutes to find the box and another four minutes to match up an old charger cord with the dead phone. Finally, he raced back up to his room, attached the phone to the cable, and plugged the cord into the outlet next to his desk. A cheesy little "charging" icon appeared on the phone's screen. *This thing really is ancient,* he thought as he sat down in the chair by his desk. *Did Tyler just think it was fancy because it's so weird-looking?*

A few minutes later Ava walked into the room. Her clothes were still filthy, but her skin was scrubbed and her hair was neatly tied back. "Sorry that took so long. Any luck?"

"Yeah, it's charging right now. I had to dig up one of my dad's old phone cords . . ."

Ava came over to the desk and hopped up on top of it. She swung her legs casually as if she hung out in Nick's room all the time. "Good job. Yeesh, it has a QWERTY keypad? If this *isn't* Marcus Hall's phone and we can't figure out who the real owner is, maybe we can sell it as an antique." She picked up the phone and pressed the power button. The screen instantly lit up. "Looks like it has just enough juice to turn on—at least if we keep it plugged in."

Ava held the phone at an angle that gave Nick a view of the screen. It had a generic wallpaper background and just a few basic icons. Suddenly the phone started buzzing with a flurry of incoming texts. Nick saw a notification pop up on the screen, saying that there were sixteen unread messages.

Ava pressed some buttons on the keypad and pulled up the text feature.

"Uh, what are you doing?" Nick asked.

"Invading the owner's privacy by checking the recent texts," said Ava matter-of-factly. Over her shoulder, Nick caught a glimpse of the unread messages. The list of senders was pretty consistent: *Mom, Mom, Mom, Mom, Mom . . .* He could only see a short preview of each message, but the most recent one began with *HONEY, WHERE ARE . . .*

Farther down the list, Nick saw a text that started with *Hey Marcus, will you . . .*

"So this *is* Marcus's phone," said Ava.

Nick's stomach clenched. "And his parents don't know where he is."

"Well, we don't know how recently these texts were sent," Ava pointed out. "Everything just says 'received at 5:47' because that's when we turned the phone back on. It's possible that

Marcus's parents were texting him this morning, and then this afternoon he came home. He could be with them right now for all we know."

"There's an easy way to find out," Nick said.

Ava was already punching at the keypad again. "I'll read off his mom's number and you can call her on your phone. Ready?"

Ready to call a complete stranger because we're worried her son might be hurt, or in danger, or . . . ? "Uh, sure."

/////

Mrs. Hall answered her phone on the first ring. "Hello?"

Nick put her on speakerphone so that Ava could hear too. "Hi, Mrs. Hall? This is Nick Morino—I'm a student at Mason Falls High School and this is kind of weird, but I'm calling to see if your son's doing okay."

"My son? You know Marcus?"

"I—sort of—not really—we have some mutual acquaintances. And he wasn't at school today so we wanted to check that nothing's wrong, and . . ."

Mrs. Hall let out a long, low moan—which didn't seem like a promising sign. "I can't believe this is happening. My husband and I haven't been able to reach him, but I just thought his phone had died. He forgets to charge it all the time, and it's such an old phone . . ."

"When was the last time you saw him?" Nick asked, feeling like a bad imitation of a TV cop.

"Yesterday morning when he left for school. He texted us yesterday evening, saying that he was staying over at a friend's house, but I don't know which friend . . . Then this morning the school called me and said he wasn't there today. And my husband and I didn't have any luck getting hold of him."

Nick glanced at Ava, who was chewing viciously on a fingernail. *The school would've called about Marcus's absence early this morning,* Nick thought. *Probably nine at the latest. And Marcus posted that photo at 10:48—so his phone definitely hadn't died at that point.* It looked like Mrs. Hall was right. Her son must've been deliberately ignoring her texts and calls, even before his phone lost power.

"So of course I've been worried since then," Mrs. Hall went on in a shaky voice. "But we kept thinking he'd be home when it got dark . . ." Her words trailed off and turned into a sob. "I don't know where he is. I don't know if he's okay. I've been on the verge of calling the police and reporting him missing, but my husband keeps telling me that's premature. Do any of his classmates have *any* idea where he could've gone?"

Nick braced himself to give her the bad news. "Well, my friend and I happened to find a phone in the forest preserve, near the falls. We're pretty sure it's Marcus's."

Mrs. Hall gasped. "Oh no. Oh *no*. Where? Do you have it? Where exactly was it? I'm calling the police *right now* . . ."

Nick told her as much as he could about their discovery and the rest of their search. Then he let her hang up to call the police.

CHAPTER 10

"What do we do now?" Ava asked.

From behind them, Nick's dad's voice startled them both. "You sit tight."

Nick and Ava whipped around. Mr. Morino was standing in the bedroom doorway, arms crossed, face grim. He looked as if he'd overheard most of Nick's conversation with Mrs. Hall.

"I wish you'd told me what was going on, Nick," he said. "We could've gotten in touch with that boy's mom much sooner."

"Sorry," said Nick. "I just—we weren't really sure if we were going overboard, inventing a crisis out of nothing. Until we found Marcus's phone."

"Right. Near the falls, you said. I'm not going to ask where *exactly* you found it. Judging by the state of Ava's clothes, it wasn't just sitting in the middle of one of the walking trails."

Nick shot a guilty look at Ava. But she just looked straight at Mr. Morino and said steadily, "We'll be happy to tell the police exactly where it was, if that'll help them target their search for Marcus."

Mr. Morino sighed, but some of the sternness left his expression. He even looked a little amused that Ava had been so ready with a comeback. *He always did like Ava*, Nick thought.

"Well, I'm sure the police will be contacting you soon," said Nick's dad. "In the meantime, we'll just have to wait and hope for the best. Dinner will be ready in fifteen minutes, by the way. That's what I came up here to tell you. And Ava, don't take this the wrong way, but I'm a little worried about that mud getting on my chairs. Nick, why don't you lend her a pair of shorts and a T-shirt?"

Nick felt his face turn hot. He was pretty sure this was *not* a typical way to start a guy-girl friendship. But he was also pretty sure he had some stuff that would fit Ava comfortably . . .

As soon as Mr. Morino left the room, Ava picked up Marcus's phone again.

"Uh, Ava? Are you back to Operation Invade a Random Kid's Privacy?"

"Like you're one to judge." She held down a button on the keypad, scrolling. "I just want to check the time of the last received text, before all the ones that came in just now. That'll give us a better idea of when his phone died . . . Oh." She blinked. "Oh man."

"What?" Nick leaned closer to see the screen better. Ava had pulled up a text draft. The intended recipients were labeled *Mom* and *Dad*.

The unsent text was short and to the point: *Don't come looking for me.*

Nick could feel the hairs on his arms stand up. The words were so stark, so dramatic, so—final. "I guess it's safe to say he was running away from home."

"Or at least he didn't want to be around his parents for a while," said Ava.

Well, that's not exactly great news, but it's better than the alternatives, Nick thought. *It means Marcus isn't hurt or in danger—he's just in hiding. Except . . .* "That doesn't explain how his phone ended up at the edge of the falls."

"I guess it's possible that he ditched it so that he'd be harder to track down. You know, lots of phones have some form of location tracking on them."

"I don't think that makes sense," said Nick. "Who runs away from home without a phone? How would he know where he was going if he couldn't look at a map? How would he find the nearest fast food place where he could grab some fries and use the restroom? How would he check the forecast and figure out if the weather would be nice enough for him to sleep outside?"

"I mean," said Ava dryly, "people ran away from home before cell phones were invented."

"Sure, because *nobody* had a cell phone and that was normal. People, like, navigated by the stars and stuff."

Ava scrunched up her face. She looked as if she was deciding whether this was an appropriate time to laugh at him.

"But anyway," said Nick, getting back on track, "if he got rid of his phone on purpose, why didn't he send that text first?"

"Easy," said Ava. "The phone died. And he probably forgot to bring his charger with him and didn't want to go back home to get it. So he figured, whatever, might as well just chuck the phone."

"Right," said Nick, unconvinced. "In the middle of a forest preserve that's full of 'Do not litter' signs. I'm not saying Marcus Hall isn't a rule breaker, but he clearly appreciates nature."

Ava sighed. "Okay, you've got me there. He probably would've tossed it in a trash can if he was getting rid of it on purpose."

"Thank you!" Nick said triumphantly. Then he remembered that they weren't having this debate for fun. A jolt of uneasiness shot through him. "So that means . . ."

"Something happened to him that made him leave it there," Ava finished for him.

"And made it impossible for him to go back for it." The full impact of the situation hit Nick like a gut punch. Whatever Marcus had been *planning* to do—wherever he'd been planning to be—there was no way to be sure what had actually happened to him after he'd uploaded that last photo at 10:48. He might be phoneless but safe, purposely lying low. Or he might be in a lot of trouble, with no way to contact anyone or reach help.

CHAPTER 11

Ava pulled out her own phone and started typing. "Social media," she said matter-of-factly. "We can put out a call for information. It's the kind of thing the police will do, except it'll be faster and better targeted."

"Good idea," Nick agreed. He woke up his laptop and went to the profile he used most often. Quickly he typed out a public post. *Mason Falls people: If anyone has seen 8th-grader Marcus Hall in the past 24 hours, please direct message me. His family is looking for him. We're hoping he's safe. Any info welcome.*

Almost instantly, someone commented on the post. It was Kayden, Kammy's little brother. *Hope you find him!*

A stream of other well wishes appeared below Kayden's comment.

Marcus has always been nice to me. I hope he's okay.

I hope this isn't because of our project for history class. I put a lot of pressure on him. I really hope he's all right.

Nick thought to himself, *I wish Marcus could see this. And if we find him—when we find him—I hope all these people keep caring about him.*

/////

Ava was in the bathroom changing into Nick's spare workout clothes. Nick was staring at Marcus Hall's phone, which was still plugged into the wall, slowly charging. Something was still bothering Nick about this phone. Especially after the time he'd just spent on social media.

He picked it up and clumsily used the keypad to navigate the screen. There were icons for texts, voicemail, contacts, an alarm clock . . . But no browser. No apps. There was nothing in the settings to show that the phone could connect to a Wi-Fi network . . . or any kind of network.

"Ava!" Nick shouted. "This isn't a smartphone!"

Ava came back into the bedroom, swimming in Nick's T-shirt and shorts. "What was that? I couldn't really hear you from the bathroom."

"This phone doesn't connect to the Internet," Nick told her.

She made a face. "Not surprising."

"But that means Marcus couldn't have used it to post his photos online," Nick said, getting more agitated by the second. "At least not without uploading them to a computer first."

"But this is definitely Marcus's phone," said Ava, puzzled.

Nick thought back to the conversations he'd had at lunchtime. "This kid named Tyler said Marcus had a fancy phone—or, wait . . . he said Marcus had a fancy *camera*."

Before Ava could respond, Nick turned to his computer, clicked on the comment Kayden had posted on his page, and searched Kayden's list of friends until he found Tyler's profile. He fired off a quick direct message to Tyler.

Hey, it's Nick—Kayden's sister's boyfriend. Sorry to bother you again, but do you happen to remember what kind of camera Marcus uses to take pictures?

Tyler must've been online and bored, because he responded immediately. *I don't know what kind it was specifically. It just looked intense, like one of those cameras that can connect to Wi-Fi and has a zillion different settings and stuff.*

Ava was reading the exchange over Nick's shoulder, following along. "You think Marcus had a camera that could do direct uploads to the Internet?"

"It would explain a lot," said Nick. He shot off a *Thanks!* to Tyler.

"Yeah," said Ava slowly, looking concerned again. "But is that really important? It doesn't actually change anything."

"The only thing it changes," Nick said, "is where we think that last photo was taken."

"I'm still not following you," said Ava. She moved away from Nick's desk to sit in the extra chair by the window.

Nick thumb-typed and arrow-buttoned his way down through Marcus's texts. "We've thought all along that Marcus's last known location is the falls. Finding his phone there seemed to confirm that. But Marcus could've lost the phone at any point."

He finally found what he was looking for: the last text Marcus had actually sent from this phone. "To be more specific: he could've lost the phone at any point after 3:07 yesterday, when he texted his parents, *Staying at my friend Luke's tonight.*"

He looked up at Ava, who was biting her nails again. She nodded slowly. "So sometime after he sent that text, he was at the falls, and his phone ended up in the spot where we found it. But after that, he could've gone somewhere else and taken that photo with his Wi-Fi-connected camera."

Nick nodded. "And if we figure out where that photo was taken, we'll be able to pinpoint Marcus's *actual* last known location."

"Hello!" called Mr. Morino from the kitchen. "Is anybody coming or should I eat all this food by myself?"

/////

If dinner at the Morino house were a performance, Ava would be crushing it. As soon as they sat down, Nick's dad started asking Ava how her parents were, what she was doing at school, her plans for the summer. Ava had always been good at talking to adults. Nick couldn't help but be impressed at how she managed to answer all his dad's questions politely and even amusingly. But he could only half-listen. He was still thinking about Marcus.

If he wasn't in the forest preserve when he took that photo, where was he? Where else does he like to hang out?

"I was planning on just living a life of sloth this summer," Ava was informing Nick's dad. "Other than going to an outrageously expensive concert in July."

"Oh yeah?" said Mr. Morino. "What group? I'm sure I've never heard of them but tell me what they're called anyway."

"It's called Bored of Education. Spelled b-o-r-e-d. I've liked them for a while, but over the past couple years they've gotten huge out of nowhere . . ."

Something lodged in Nick's brain. *Wait a minute . . . Bored . . . Board . . .*

"Be right back," he said, bolting up from the table.

Back in his room, he slid into his desk chair and woke up his laptop. Ava dashed in right behind him, out of breath. "What's up?"

"One second." He typed *Mason Falls skate park* into his search engine and then clicked on the image results. After he'd scrolled down about half a page, he found what he was hoping to see.

"I've got an idea about where Marcus might be."

CHAPTER 12

Nick pointed to the image on the computer screen. It was a photo of the local skate park. And it clearly showed the edge of a ramp decorated with the swirling blue-and-purple bird graffiti they'd been trying to find.

"At 10:48 this morning," Nick told Ava, "Marcus Hall was at the skate park."

"How'd you figure that out? I never thought of you as the skateboarding type."

"I'm not. But Kayden's friend Tyler mentioned that he sometimes saw Marcus at the skate park taking pictures. And, if you think about it, the skate park would be a pretty decent place to hunker down if you're trying to hide out. It's still closed for the winter, so nobody else would be there. And there are lots of tubes and arches and things to block the wind or give some shelter if it rains."

Ava nodded thoughtfully. "Smarter and safer than trying to squat in the forest preserve, at least. It's worth checking out. Do you think your dad could give us a ride there?"

Nick grimaced. "He made it pretty clear that he thinks we should just stay here and wait to hear from the police."

"Yeah . . . I guess we could call the police and tell them about your hunch. Do you think they'd take us seriously?"

"Not in that outfit," Nick deadpanned.

"Hey, I work with what I'm given." Ava's eyes drifted over to the charger that was still slowly pumping life into Marcus's phone. "Speaking of which . . . I think I've got an idea."

/////

"Hey, Mr. Morino," Ava said sweetly as she and Nick helped his dad clear the table. "Nick says you've got a Commodore 64 down in your basement. I'd love to see it if it's not too much trouble. I love old computers."

"Really?" said Mr. Morino, clearly delighted. "Well, I'll pop down there and see if I can find it for you. You two can get a head start on washing these dishes while I'm looking. Feel free to put some music on . . ."

As soon as Mr. Morino had disappeared into the basement, Nick and Ava dumped the dishes in the kitchen sink. Ava turned on Mr. Morino's MP3 player and cranked it up to full blast while Nick grabbed the car keys from the magnetic holder on the fridge.

"He'll be down there for at least half an hour," Nick whispered as they slipped through the door to the attached garage. He had no idea how long this was going to take. But if they could at least get out of the house without Mr. Morino noticing, Nick would take the rest of it one step at a time.

"The great thing about this car is how quiet it is," Nick added as he unlocked the driver's door. "We'll be able to make a silent getaway. Assuming Dad doesn't hear the garage door open."

"I don't think we have to worry about that," Ava noted as the music blaring from the MP3 player swelled even louder. "I wouldn't have guessed your dad was a heavy metal guy."

"Yeah," said Nick. "We Morinos are full of surprises."

///////

Dusk was setting in as Nick drove toward the skate park. "Should we at least call Mrs. Hall?" Ava asked.

Nick shook his head. "Let's wait and see if we actually find him there. Or evidence that he's been there. No point in getting her worked up if it turns out to be a dead end."

Ava nodded. "Good point."

"But I really hope we're right about this," Nick added. "Because if we're not, my dad will *never* let me drive again."

CHAPTER 13

After Nick parked the car, he and Ava walked up to the hulking shapes of the skate park ramps. It was almost totally dark now. Nick shined his cell phone light in front of them, then cast it in a wide loop over their surroundings. Strange shapes loomed at him: the curve of a ramp, the sharp jut of a rail, a towering structure that turned out to be another ramp. Then there were the unexpected bursts of color as the light caught bits of graffiti. And the even more unexpected drop-off where the concrete surface dipped into a bowl. Nick made a mental note to stay clear of the bowl's edge.

"Marcus?" Nick called out quietly. "Are you here?"

Ava whispered, "This is creepy. What if someone shifty is hanging out here?"

"Now you're sounding like me."

"Yeah, I guess you've rubbed off on me. Maybe we should be really quiet and just listen for a minute."

"Works for me."

They waited, breathing shallowly. Nick kept shining his phone light around. Ramp, ledge, set of stairs, ramp, vertical wall, ramp . . .

Was that a rustling noise?

"Did you hear that?" Ava hissed.

"Yeah—where'd it come from?"

"Over there, I think—in that tunnel thing."

She was pointing to the tube on the far side of the giant hole in the ground.

Nick heard a scraping sound, followed by a hiss. *That could be a human voice, or . . .* His brain ran through a list of all the wildlife that roamed the forest preserve and the surrounding area. *I do not want to have to explain to my dad that I stole his car and then got attacked by an angry raccoon . . .*

"Turn off your phone light," Ava whispered.

"Um, that's a terrible idea," Nick whispered back. "What if someone shifty is there, like you said before? Or some kind of wild animal?"

"*Or* what if Marcus is there, and he makes a run for it when he realizes we're heading his way?"

Nick considered for a moment. "Okay. But we have to be really careful to avoid that bowl. We did not survive Mason Falls just to end up breaking our necks falling into a skating pit."

"Deal," Ava agreed.

Nick turned off the light.

They crept as silently as possible toward the tube, giving the yawning hole a wide berth. They came at the tube from the side, and as they got closer, Ava motioned to Nick with her hand. Nick had to squint to see her gestures in the darkness, but he quickly figured out what she meant. *I'll take that end, you take the other end.*

Nick nodded. They would each go for an opening, blocking both exits in case whoever was inside the tube tried to flee. *But if it turns out to be a rabid animal—or even, like, a rogue graffiti artist—all bets are off.*

Ava peeled off toward the left opening. Nick headed for the one on the right. At the same time, they both peered into the concrete tube, and Nick turned on his phone light again.

The light shone on a scrawny kid huddling in the center of the tube, clutching his backpack to his chest.

The Kid let out a yelp of surprise and terror. So did Nick.

"It's okay!" Ava shouted over both of them. "Marcus! It's okay! We're just here to help!"

Nick quickly got hold of himself. A moment later Marcus fell silent too, though his head swiveled frantically from Nick to Ava. He looked as if he were deciding whether to throw his backpack at one of them.

"Who are you?" Marcus rasped out in a shaky voice.

"Oh! Right." Nick had forgotten—again—that Marcus didn't actually know them. "I'm Nick and this is Ava. We, uh . . ."

"We've been helping your parents look for you," offered Ava. "They've been really worried." *Man, she's smooth,* thought Nick.

Even in the weak light from his phone, Nick could see Marcus's shoulders relax and the distrust fade from his expression. "I thought you were—I don't know." His fear was clearly changing to embarrassment.

"Sorry we spooked you," said Ava. "Are you okay?"

"Um—yeah, mostly."

Nick and Ava exchanged a glance, even though they could barely see each other's faces in the dark. "*Mostly?*" Nick echoed.

"Well, I can't really walk very well. I was up by the falls earlier today, and I tripped and hurt my ankle. I don't think it's broken, just twisted. Anyway, I was able to walk on it for a while, but by the time I got here it was hurting a lot more."

"We have my dad's car," said Nick. "We can take you home."

Marcus gave him a withering look. "Why should I get in a car with random people I don't know?"

Oh. Good point. I've spent the past day worrying about this kid's safety, and now I look like the most threatening thing he's run into.

"I've got your mom's number," Ava said. "I'll call her and make sure it's okay with her if we drive you. Does that work?"

Marcus hesitated, but only for another second. Then he nodded and started to crawl out of the pipe toward Ava.

He only had his backpack with him. Ava shouldered it while Nick helped Marcus stand up. With Ava and Nick on either side of him, supporting him, he limped out of the skate park toward Mr. Morino's car.

/////

Ava called Mrs. Hall immediately to let her know that Marcus was safe. Meanwhile Marcus gave Nick his mom's address, and Nick plugged it into his GPS and took off down the street.

"Your parents are going to kill you," Ava informed Marcus after she ended the call with Mrs. Hall.

"I figured," said Marcus in a hollow voice.

"You're not alone," Nick assured him. "My dad's not going to be thrilled that I took his car without his permission. But at least it was for a good cause, right?"

He watched Marcus's face in the rearview mirror, hoping to get a smile out of him, but no luck.

Nick figured they had no right to ask Marcus to explain himself, but he was dying to know what had set this off. What Marcus had been running from yesterday. What had scared and upset him so badly.

Ava reached into the small purse she'd brought with her. "By the way, I think this belongs to you." She took out Marcus's clunky little phone and handed it to him.

"Oh man, I thought I'd lost it!"

"You did lose it," Ava said matter-of-factly. "We found it over by the falls."

"Yeah, I dropped it when I tripped. I was so

freaked out about my ankle that I didn't even notice at first. And then by the time I realized it was gone, I was halfway to the skate park and my foot was really starting to hurt. So I didn't try to go back."

"Well, I'm sure your parents will be glad to know you weren't blowing them off on purpose," Ava said. "At least not the *whole* day." Nick was impressed that she somehow kept any hint of judgment out of her voice.

"Well, I wasn't trying to run away forever or anything." Marcus sounded a little sulky now. "That's little-kid stuff. I just couldn't deal with my parents. I had this huge fight with them on Wednesday night . . ."

He paused and swallowed heavily. Nick was surprised at how much Marcus had said already. Clearly, he wasn't always as quiet and closed-up as he seemed around his classmates.

"My mom told me she's going to send me to private school next year," Marcus went on. "Over in Silver Valley. I'd have to take the bus for an hour each way. And I wouldn't know *anyone* there. I mean, it's not like I'm popular here, but at least everyone's familiar, you know?"

"Sure," said Ava. "There's nothing wrong with liking what's familiar." She glanced at Nick, then quickly looked away. "On the other hand, you never know if you'll like something new until you try it. The other school could surprise you."

She said it casually, in the same tone she used with Nick. Not talking down to him, not treating him like some little kid who needed to be comforted—just stating her point of view. It didn't seem to improve Marcus's outlook, though. He slumped in the backseat and stared glumly out the window.

Nick thought of Josh again. Josh hadn't made any friends at *his* private school. That probably wasn't the school's fault, but it also told Nick that a change of location might not be enough to make Marcus happy.

"So you had a fight about that on Wednesday night," Nick prompted him. "And then yesterday . . ."

Marcus shrugged, still gazing out the window. "I guess I kind of panicked. After school I ran home and packed a bunch of stuff, and then I went to the skate park to hide out."

"And you texted your parents that you were staying over at a friend's place."

A grudging nod from Marcus.

"So you've been out on your own since last night?" asked Ava.

"It wasn't so bad," said Marcus a little defensively. "Until today, when my phone died and I twisted my ankle. But I had plenty of food and water and deodorant and stuff."

"Oh, well, as long as you had deodorant," said Ava with a straight face.

An awkward silence fell. Nick glanced at the GPS. *You will reach your destination in seven minutes.*

Great. Seven whole minutes.

"Do you like Bored of Education?" Ava asked Marcus suddenly.

"What's that?"

Ava grinned at him and started tapping on her phone. "Oh, sir, your life is about to change for the better."

They spent the next seven minutes listening to Ava's favorite band. Nick noticed that Marcus was nodding along with the beat. And for the first time the Kid looked as if he might be capable of smiling.

CHAPTER 14

Marcus's parents were beyond relieved to see him. Nick and Ava planned to make a quick exit, but Mrs. Hall insisted that they come inside.

Once the Halls had calmed down, Marcus hobbled off to take a shower. Mr. Hall called the police to tell them Marcus had been found. Mrs. Hall herded her awkward guests into the kitchen and forced cans of soda into their hands.

"I can't thank you enough," she said. "We knew he was upset about switching schools next year, but we never expected him to do something like this. And we never would've known where to look for him."

"Does he—does he *have* to switch schools next year, Mrs. Hall?" Nick asked, hoping he didn't sound incredibly rude.

She sighed. "He's not exactly thriving at Mason Falls Middle School. All his teachers describe him as a loner. I can't imagine that the high school will be much better for him. It'll be all the same students."

Nick heard footsteps outside the kitchen and realized that the shower had stopped running. Marcus was probably overhearing this conversation. He raised his voice just a little. "Well, if it's the other students you're worried about, I know a great kid named Kayden who's in Marcus's grade. Maybe they'll have a class together next year. And a bunch of other kids have been asking about him, saying they hope he's okay. They seem like good guys. Even Wyatt Rosen's not that bad, as long as Marcus does half of their history project."

Mrs. Hall gave him a blank look. "I'm not sure what you're trying to say, young man."

"What I'm trying to say is—maybe give

Marcus one more year at Mason Falls. Things can change a lot in high school. I mean, there's a photography class he can take. He might make some friends that way. And Ava and I will still be at the high school next year. I bet Marcus wouldn't mind a couple of cool seniors looking out for him."

"So we'll try to find a couple of cool seniors," Ava joked.

Still not much of a reaction from Mrs. Hall. Nick knew he didn't have the right to lecture her, so he finished up quickly. "I just think he might have a better shot at making friends at Mason Falls than at a completely unfamiliar school. It might be worth it to give him a chance. And give *us* a chance to make him feel welcome."

Mrs. Hall let out a long, exhausted breath. "I'll think about it. Thank you again for everything, both of you."

"Glad we could help," said Ava. Nick tried to hide his disappointment that his dramatic speech hadn't completely convinced her.

On their way to the front door, they passed

Marcus, who gave Nick a small smile.

"Thanks," Marcus said, nodding toward the kitchen where his mom was waiting for him. Nick could tell he had been listening carefully.

"No problem." Nick gave him a quick pat on the shoulder. "Hang in there."

"We'll see you around," added Ava, and Marcus's smile grew.

/////

"Weird night," said Nick as he drove home.

"Yup," said Ava absentmindedly, tapping at her phone.

"Want me to drop you off at your place?"

"I think I left my backpack at your house," Ava said. "And, um, my clothes." She glanced down at the T-shirt and shorts she'd changed into. "It *miiiiight* send the wrong message to my parents if I show up wearing your clothes."

Nick couldn't decide whether to be mortified or amused, so the sound that came out of his mouth was a choked laugh.

Ava seemed to be biting back a smile too. "I can just grab my stuff and change at your place, and then walk home from there."

"Good," said Nick. "Because as soon as we get there I'll probably be banned from driving this thing until I turn thirty."

Back at Nick's house, the MP3 player in the kitchen was still blasting. Mr. Morino was nowhere in sight.

"He must still be in the basement!" Nick whispered in awe. It had to be almost an hour since they'd sneaked out. Nick had been sure his dad would've noticed they were gone by now. Apparently his dad was really invested in his search for that computer for Ava.

Ava put her hand over her mouth to smother a laugh. "Aww, it's so sweet that he wants to find that Commodore 64 for me. Tell him I said thanks, okay?"

Nick hovered awkwardly in the front hallway while Ava got changed in the bathroom. Within two minutes she was back, wearing her dirt-covered clothes again.

"Thanks for the loan," she said, handing him his folded shorts and shirt.

"No problem. Just don't tell Jeff Groves."

She laughed and picked up her backpack.

"Hey, thank you—for everything," Nick added. "I never would've tracked down Marcus without your help."

Ava shrugged. "You're the one who was convinced something was up with him. And you were right. I'm glad I eventually listened to you." Shouldering her backpack, she reached for the doorknob. "See you Monday."

Nick took a deep breath. "Actually, Kammy's having a thing at her mom's house tomorrow night—seven thirty. If you're interested. She said to invite you. And . . . I think it'd be cool if you came. You could bring Dan."

Ava thought about that for a second. "Thanks. I might. Can you give me Kammy's number?"

"Oh, sure." He pulled out his phone and texted her his girlfriend's number.

"Thanks. Oh hey, take a look at this," she said, handing him her phone. He glanced down at the screen, which showed a new notification. *Josh Adler has accepted your friend request.*

"Whoa! You found Josh?"

"Yup. He's got super intense privacy settings, so that's why we could never find him before. He was basically unsearchable."

Unsearchable—yeah, that sounded about right. Losing track of people was easy. Rediscovering them tended to be a lot harder.

"So how did you end up finding him?"

"Well, while we were in the car listening to Bored of Education, I did a basic search for his name and found out he plays for the Silver Valley baseball team. So I texted Dan and asked him to ask his friends on the baseball team if Josh's name rang a bell. Dan texted me back that his friend Bryce knew Josh. Turned out Josh had friended Bryce at some point, so then *I* friended Bryce, and *then* I was able to find Josh's profile. Anyway, now we can get back in touch with him."

"That's great," said Nick, impressed. "And you did all that in the seven minutes it took to get to Marcus's house?"

"Had to make up for lost time." She flashed him a grin. "Now give me back my phone so I can go home."

He obediently handed the phone back to her. She tucked it into her pocket and headed for the door.

"Hey, Ava?"

"Yup?" she said over her shoulder.

"I'm glad we're friends again." He hoped he didn't sound too dramatic.

Ava just grunted in response. But this time, Nick had a pretty good idea what she meant.

MASON FALLS MYSTERIES

BEHIND THE SCREEN
THE HOUSE
TRACKS
THE TURNAROUND

EVEN AN ORDINARY TOWN
HAS ITS SECRETS.

DAY OF DISASTER

Would you survive?

ABOUT THE AUTHOR

Vanessa Acton is a writer and editor in Minneapolis, Minnesota. She enjoys stalking dead people (also known as historical research), drinking too much tea, and taking long walks during her home state's annual three-week thaw.